VIRTUAL DEATH

AN INSPECTOR MARTINET MYSTERY

DAVID FARREN

Also by David Farren

NONFICTION

The Return of Magic (1972)
Living with Magic (1974)
Sex and Magic (1975)
Finding Magic (2001)

FICTION

Mendaga's Morning (1979)
Redeeming the Cisco Kid (2013)
Crazy in Los Angeles (2013)
Hall the Viking (2013)
The Witches of Westwood (2019)
Red Sky at Night (2021)

ISBN: 9798794304374
Imprint: Independently published

I

Fran Martinet had been allowed the rest of the week off. She felt it was only her due. She could sleep late, enjoy time with her extended family, and welcome in 2027 by herself. The short-handed SFPD had been barely keeping up with the holiday homicides.

Since she was still just one of a handful of female officers, Fran had been getting more than her fair share of the cases where women were the alleged perps. Most of them were routine enough that a single trip to the station at the edge of Golden Gate Park broke the case.

Women seemed to feel it was a lot easier to confess to another woman. Fran could understand that since some years before she had been in much the same situation as many of them, desperate souls who had forcibly removed a violent male from their lives.

She had done this herself years earlier. She broke the neck of a cheating boyfriend when she tossed him off the balcony of her condo overlooking the Pampers Stadium ball field.

Fran had not asked for a lawyer. Given her JD from Cal back

when the law school was still named after the genocidal real estate tycoon Serranus Clinton Hastings, she knew the routine well enough. It was quite simple: shut the fudge up and see if they'd let her go.

She had perhaps broken a record in getting back to her life. It helped that two other people had been in the room when cheating boyfriend came at her with a samurai sword that had decorated her wall. She had been standing in the doorway to the balcony.

It was an easy move to sidestep him in such a way that his momentum carried him to the railing. She made sure he kept going. Self-defense, pure and simple.

What happened wasn't held against her when she applied to be a cop six years back. It had been at a time when the pandemic and morale-busting limits on law enforcement had taken its toll on the department. She was welcomed, especially by the DEIA monitor on its payroll.

Three years later she had moved from plain clothes to detective. San Francisco was unique in following the European usage of referring to them as inspectors. Earlier the rank and its pay were equivalent to being a lieutenant in any other part of the state. Now it was the same as that of a sergeant.

Introducing herself as Inspector Martinet always had an effect, especially to British visitors fond of Ruth Rendell's Inspector

Wexford or any number of characters on the telly.

There would be plenty of action since it was the night before the new year of 2027. She had been in front of her wall-size set watching the celebrations as the witching hour took its westward path from Australia to New York. In Times Square the ball was about to drop when her phone buzzed. She pushed a button on the arm of her chair and answered the call.

Yes, it had been too good to be true. Her respite from police work was cut short by a call to get over ASAP to the metaverse playground at O'Farrell and Van Ness.

II

Problems at a metaverse playground normally didn't require a one-eight-seven call, and definitely not one to an officer suspended for how she had handled the last gift from the gods in RHD. But then Captain Quine had disagreed with Internal Affairs on that one. He had a fondness for mavericks like her. It reminded him of the way things had been for Bullitt and Dirty Harry, at least in the movies.

He liked to joke, somewhat offensively, that his mom and Mary were alike in giving birth to a true messiah. His promised kingdom, though, was in heaven only in the metaphorical sense of residing in "the cloud" as he devoted himself to increasing the use of AR (augmented reality) in police work.

Fran had been invited to take part in a demonstration SFPD put on to acquaint their personnel of possible applications to police work. She was not impressed. So far it seemed just another addition to a list of ersatz products, like vegan steaks and non-alcoholic whiskey.

Already there were too many simulations. They ranged from when to shoot so that she would not pop an innocent citizen to how to avoid anything that could possibly be construed as ethnic or gender harassment. Good intentions all, but not a substitute for actual experience.

She snorted when offered the latest Robbie the Robot to ride with her and help out with witness interrogations. Quine said it would make sure she asked the right questions for the field interrogation form. She snapped back that his being there would keep her from getting the right answers.

"We can have him come in chocolate," he suggested. That's when she went over and "accidentally" knocked his hot coffee into the waste basket.

As a self-assured Black woman, no white male had permission to use any word suggesting her color irreverently. Quine should have known better. She had let him get off easy.

II

Metaverse playgrounds, which began developing as the virtual gaming industry looked for new ways to milk the public, were intended for family entertainment. During the early Covid days, when staying home was sometimes a requirement, the VR industry had come into its own.

At one time, gaming had been limited to increasingly sophisticated apps for desktops and tablets. Much of the industry profit came from selling freemiums, particularly extra in-game content that gave the savvy player a competitive edge in games that could take weeks to complete, but this itself limited the number of purchasers. One wit compared it to the difference between street racing with an expensive souped-up hotrod and going for a joy ride on a second-hand bicycle.

Fran had been a toddler when Japan, which had been first in the market with smart phones, unleashed gaming consoles on the world. Headphones gave way to clumsy skull-embracing headsets that, linked with downloaded software, allowed the sense of actual first-person experiences in a simulated environment.

AR (augmented reality) with its specialized glasses or goggles was for both work and play. VR (virtual reality) was primarily for play, but by 2020 its place as a multibillion-dollar piece of her nation's economy was well established. The key to increasing revenue was the need to subscribe to a service that kept the games—and their enhancements—coming.

The most recent jump had been from home-based entertainment with play stations to what quickly came to be called playgrounds. They opened up the market by providing places where a full virtual reality experience could be rented by the hour so that occasional players no longer needed to possess equipment that cost a bundle and a half. The goal was to make VR gaming more like going to Disneyland but without the travel and some very expensive tickets.

Ambitious, well-heeled entrepreneurs began buying office buildings emptied by the remote work movement. Office pods were transformed into enclosed play stations with all the enhancements expected by serious gamers. They were also expected to be family friendly. G and PG games were the only ones provided, but that was just when things were getting started.

No Limits had entered the market when the corporation took over the old O'Farrell theater on the edge of the Tenderloin. Back in 1969 James and Artie Miller had begun with a strip club, then expanded into showing porn when it was still very illegal to do so. They had taken advantage of various loopholes that allowed them to show the pornography then produced in Denmark, which had decriminalized it and found its availability very much reduced peeping-tom offenses.

A Supreme Court ruling then eviscerated most laws against pornography by saying that any case should be decided in terms of community standards. The one exception, by federal law, was so-called kiddie porn, enough to ruin careers when found on someone's computer.

Predictably, a No Limits Club, as it was called, was strictly R. It was for clients—no one was to be addressed with such a demeaning term as "customer"—who had an itch for more edgy experiences, and No Limits programmers aimed to please.

Anyone familiar with San Francisco lore would remember that in 1990 James Mitchell went to his younger brother's home in an effort to have "party Artie" give up drinking and, above all, give up the guns he had acquired and often brandished about. He broke down the door and found Arthur Mitchell coming at him with a gun.

He claimed he had just fired his own gun into the ceiling and did not recall the shot that killed his brother. The conviction was for manslaughter rather than murder, but even after the older brother's death in 1990 it was hard to forget what had happened. Fran was aware of rumors that Artie's ghost still roamed the area, especially in Little Saigon just to the South along Larkin Avenue.

This one-eight-seven was already spooking Fran as she rolled out to Third Street. What if this meant she had to deal with Artie's ghost. No, her homicides had never yet had supernatural overtones, unless one was to count the phony psychic who overplayed her hand out by the Cliff House eight years ago, well before she had been with SFPD.

IV

Fran had a distinctive advantage in her appearance. Six-one with a shaved skull (something inspired long back by the actress Jada Pinkett), a light cocoa complexion thanks to an Algerian mother and a Haitian father, she would be recognized even if she were not wearing one of her Hermes cashmere jumpsuits. Being plain-clothes did not have to mean not standing out, impossible in this city where she was already something of a celebrity.

The cop handling the door to the playground spotted her right off and waved her in.

Each floor above the entrance and client lounge had several rows of roomy cubicles, each shut off from floor to ceiling with opaque bullet-proof glass. There was a commissary of sorts with beverages and branded packs of marijuana cigarettes available at the clients' disposal.

Some clients imagined certain extra services but that wasn't going to happen. The management of No Limit Enterprises, the corporation that had decided to challenge Mark Zuckerbergs's intended monopoly of the metaverse, wanted this to remain a class act. That's what the old O'Farrell theater had tried to be when the gonzo journalist Hunter Thompson deemed it "the Carnegie Hall of public sex in America."

By the time she had arrived, other patrons had been refunded their money and given free vouchers for some time in the future. She was escorted to the scene of the crime on the third floor.

Two kids from Cal had used a voucher to rent World C3. The deceased was Jaime Morales and the presumed perp was his brother, Arturo Morales.

Fran had listened to their names before she went in. She immediately recognized they were the Hispanic versions of the names James and Arthur.

Her immediate reaction was in keeping with what she had learned to expect from her boss. "This better not be one of Quine's practical jokes. If so, I'm going to kick his ass."

The cop standing there was obviously puzzled.

"Hell no, Inspector. We had one very dead customer who's now in the morgue. We kept the other guy here because someone downtown said to. He said he was going to call you."

Fran knew by now that they'd be wrapping up the show from

Manhattan. At first, she had the wild thought that whoever did this to her had to be someone who knew, unlike Quine, that she loved to watch the New Year's show on CNN because she had a cousin out there laughing it up. It was the only time of the year he'd be drinking during a show, and sometimes things slipped out. She could rib him about it all the way to the summer.

It had to be a coincidence, like the fact that the brothers here happened to have the same first names as the Mitchell brothers, but with the twist that now it was Artie who had stabbed Jim.

V

There was a private section of the guest lounge downstairs set aside for patrons who might become indisposed. That was something quite possible with some of the simulated adventures, and for that reason there was always a qualified medic, moonlighting from his day job as an EMT with SFFD, on hand. The officer with him was a woman she knew from the department, Amy Tan, now assigned to third watch as she climbed the ladder from being on the street. Captain Quine had acted on her recommendation to interview Arturo Morales here rather than downtown. Outside the room she filled Fran in on what they knew so far.

The first was that the brothers were graduate students at UC Berkeley. No Limits had promoted a lottery there and at other two-year and four-year schools in the Bay area. One student from each school would win an entirely free pass on New Year's Eve to the O'Farrell Street playground. The single restriction was that they had to be of legal age to drink. The winner could have as many as five other people share his World play station with all snacks and beverages, apart from the marijuana, complimentary. Jaime had been the winner.

Arturo was his obvious pick to share the good time ahead, but the few relatives and friends he had also called had different ideas about how to spend this final day of 2026. None of them were gamers, and Jaime himself could only remember playing Pac-Man in the lobby in at one of the movie theaters he went to as a kid.

Arturo had to cancel his date with the girl he had been seeing off and on, but then Jaime was his big brother and best friend and a guy who had never in his life really cut loose. Jaime had been so damn lucky to have a chance to do so now, even it was just virtually.

They had arrived a little after six. Both had to get used to what they had to do in order to get the full VR experience.

Amy handed Fran a copy of the colorful laminated brochure given all players along with various consent forms.

The most important thing about the play stations setting them apart from the competition was that they no longer needed cumbersome headsets. Instead there were snug-fitting caps reaching down to the base of the skull. The walls of the game pod itself were embedded with thousands of tiny cells for transmission to and from the incredibly tiny chips embedded in the caps.

The chips in turn, as she explained to Fran, somehow both

monitored and dictated action in all parts of the brain itself. The example cited in the brochure was how neurons in the brain both responded to actual stimuli from what we see or hear or touch and parallel stimuli from activated connections inside the cortex itself.

"This is how we both dream and hallucinate," she said. "I've been a player here for two months now. They have nailed the way to make us do it on cue with literally millions of messages from these walls each second. They package different adventures just like the traditional games that use a headset to set up something visual for your eyes and ears. Here the signals hit your brain directly. You don't really move your arms and legs, but, like a phantom limb experience, you feel as though they are there anyway."

"Not much exercise, though," Fran remarked.

"Just think of the medical applications they are already making possible, Fran. The blind can see again, for instance, just like the deaf can hear."

Fran had only one response. "So how are they to know whether what you see or hear is what the world is like or not just only how the programmers want you to see or hear it? No Limits might just be updating Orwell's vision of 1984."

Amy was clearly offended. "Damn it, Fran, why do you always have to be so negative?"

She did not ty to answer. Instead she just thought back to being a kid and having a white teenager try to brand her like a cow on his ranch. She had grabbed the red-hot iron and applied it to his crotch. His family called the police. It was a brace of Black officers who visited her parents. One of them did the song and dance, then gave her a medal from his tour in Iraq.

"Never let them break you, sugar."

So far no one had.

VI

Arturo had managed to calm down enough to do the necessary interview. He had been read his Miranda rights and he understood he might still end up in a cell with some New Year's drunks vomiting on his expensive Kobe memorial high-top sneakers.

The brothers had already played through a number of the games—scripts as No Limits preferred to describe them—available in World C3. What was curious about them was how they were so opposite the woke emphasis they had become used to in their high school years and again at Berkeley.

One had been about the chain of missions founded by Saint Junipero Serra. It was a reenactment of the imagined capture and beating of an Indian who had tried to escape from the venerated Santa Barbara Mission, once a major tourist stop in Southern California. The view rendered in Jaime's brain was supposedly that of one of the friars while in Arturo's it was that of the Indian. Both, somewhat nauseous, had exited the game in a hurry.

There was complimentary champagne for the holiday. It lightened their moods enough that in looking over the menu they decided to go with the recommended selection: "Escaping Jack the Ripper."

As in most VR games there was a proprietary setting. For this game it was the network of London streets as they would have looked to someone in the time of Queen Victoria. There were the horse-drawn carriages that could run you down, the gang of waifs eager to pick your pocket, and above all someone waiting to shove a knife in your back just for the sheer fun of it.

If you looked in a window and saw your reflection it might be that of a toff armed just with a hollow walking stick from which you could extract a thin rapier, or it might be a young female streetwalker armed with a dagger. The game itself decided who you would be and what weapons you might have available.

The object of the game was to get from Piccadilly Circus to Covent Garden, a distance that ideally could be a ten-minute walk, in the shortest time possible despite obstacles. These would include at least one encounter with Jack the Ripper, who might be disguised in any number of ways.

You were advised that you might want to play the game several times just to enjoy the setting, but each time you had to be on guard. You had extra points, translated into a cash reward at the end of your rental, if you managed to turn the tables and dispatch the Ripper rather than just escape from him.

The pod itself had translucent plexiglass dividers separating the comfortable chairs where the players were to remain while the script was running. Leaving the chair terminated the game and effectively shortened the rental time available. For the boys that did not matter since Jaime's gift rental was for the entire evening up to midnight.

They had each put on their VR caps after the champagne break and settled in their chairs. Their brains registered a soft feminine voice asking if they were ready to play. All they had to do was think "yes" or "go ahead" or anything that indicated agreement.

In the script they were each walking from Piccadilly Circus but not on the same route. Jaime and Arturo had no way of recognizing each other as they got started. According to the script monitoring system, Jaime had managed to avoid being crushed by a runaway carriage and was almost at Covent Garden when the unthinkable happened.

The monitor showed Arturo turning a corner and finding himself face to face with his brother's avatar. Jaime apparently thought he now was directly in front of the Ripper since the man he saw was holding a poniard and seemed ready to strike. He turned to run.

Arturo had also thought he had met up with the Ripper, who now was trying to escape him. His own reaction was to go for the extra points, so he leaped at the running figure and plunged his dagger into the man's unprotected neck.

The script ended instantly. The cubicle, which had remained dark while the script played on, now lit up. Arturo looked over and froze in horror. His brother was prone by his chair with blood flowing out of his neck and spreading on the floor.

A maintenance alarm went off, just as it would if a player had brought in a drink and spilled it. Arturo could not account for his actions in the two minutes between the game ending and the floor attendant rushing in to find him on his knees and gripping Jaime's shoulders in an attempt to turn him over.

VII

It would not be until the following day that one of the playground managers was able to access footage from the monitor. While it showed one avatar stabbing another it was no help in determining what had happened in the cubicle itself. If Arturo had left his chair and murdered his brother—what the floor attendant thought he had done—the game would have ended before the stabbing.

The attendant himself was a big guy who too often had to act as a bouncer when intoxicated players, not satisfied with the thrill of virtual violence, started punching each other around in the real world. Arturo found himself in plastic restraints as the attendant, who went by the improbable name of Reed Ryder and wore a Western costume, pushed him into a corner.

He saw it was too late for emergency action, but he called the house medic anyway and made him handle the 911. Two hours later and he was being interrogated, first by Amy Tan and then by Fran Martinet. He kept praying no one would think he had just killed a client, especially with the blood on his clothes.

Fran tried to reassure Ryder he was not a suspect. She still was not completely sure about Arturo, but already her hunch was that this had been a staged event. The trick was learning who and how. Then she could work on why.

Arturo was in no shape to go home, and there did not seem to be a basis for treating him as anything more than a witness. She began to think that even a tawny rather than gold C-3PO might have come in handy after all. Her own notes were incomplete, and that did not happen often.

A lot had been going through her mind even while she was attempting to concentrate on what she was hearing both from the boy and from Reed Ryder. With the latter it had been a memory of the actor Robert Blake being acquitted of murder and the trivia item that as a child actor he had played Little Beaver in a long list of Red Ryder films ground out by Republic Pictures right after the Second World War.

Finally she had Amy see what she could for the kid. Maybe Quine would be willing to dip into the budget and get Arturo a place to stay with police protection. She doubted there was much she could learn from playground management. No, go upstairs to whoever coordinated the supposed lottery.

An old but trusted rule was not to believe in mere coincidences.

Things had been rigged with the express purpose of having an Arthur kill his brother Jim at the original site of the Miller brothers theater. Forget about Arthur's ghost. There was a phantom at work, motive as yet unknown, and a couple of nice kids had been played like puppets.

With the holiday being on a Friday it was unlikely she could get hold of any No Limits people before Monday. Well, there was a lot she would have to learn about VR playgrounds and she should get going on it. Her weekend was already shot. She might as well ruin someone else's.

VIII

Jordan Tran almost did not get hired for the SFPD crime lab when he applied soon after the new building housing it was finished. He was Vietnamese and the diversity head honcho said that the Asians already were over the quota. She needed either a Pacific Islander or an Inuit from Alaska. Fortunately for Jordan the need for his specialized talents trumped wokeness.

He had been recovering from the previous night's revels at his girlfriend's apartment in the other Little Saigon down south, just a bit off the San Diego Freeway. They had tickets for the Rose Bowl and were just finishing breakfast while watching the floats roll along Colorado Boulevard.

His cell rang and immediately he knew Lily was not going to be happy. Inspector Martinet needed help. Now, she knew this would be a great imposition, but she'd try wheedling Captain Quine into making it worthwhile….

Well, this was her brother's lucky day. He could cheer on

Tommy Trojan.

Jordan managed a flight back to Oakland with minutes to spare, stopped off at his own apartment, then rode the BART back to his lab. He got to see the kickoff in Pasadena but that was it before Martinet arrived.

Fran's first question after a hurried briefing was how it might be possible to hack the game that the Morales brothers had been engaged in.

"You got the money, honey, they got the time. That's what hacking is all about. Never think you're safe. I can imagine that No Limits has competitors that would like to see them go broke. Having customers die on the premises like a crazy reenactment might appeal to some weirdos, but it's not going to keep the seats filled. You'd keep thinking you could be next. That's way too edgy."

"So humor me," Fran said. Imagine you had a reason for this set-up and somehow you heard you had a pair of boys that would be just right for it."

Jordan had his tablet out. He dictated notes.

"Point one. What are the chances of brothers with the names James and Arthur and of drinking age? Could this be hacked from college enrollment records at Cal, SF State, USF, and a few community colleges? I'm skipping the Catholic schools and the special art or theater ones."

"USF is Catholic," Fran reminded him.

"Yeah, but it's run by Jesuits, so I don't know if I should count it. Anyway, we need to find out just what schools our supposed hacker did bother with. Advertising a lottery still costs, and there has to be a way of making sure your targets in fact enter the lottery. That it's rigged we'll take for granted, and we might as well also take for granted that there has to be somebody inside No Limits doing it."

"Possibly a lottery was in the works anyway, and our hacker jumped on board for reasons still to be determined."

"Keep that open. Point two. How did someone manage to kill the one brother with the other taking the rap? The thing about what No Limits was into with a direct feed into the brain gives a whole new meaning to brainwashing. Why not feed in 'go kill your brother as soon as the script gives you a chance.' Or maybe it's that Arturo really is as innocent as it looks now. Then we have to think whether something could be fired from the wall itself."

"We're working to get an autopsy today, holiday or not," Fran said. "I'll make sure that we find whether there's anything still in Jaime's neck. And we've already sealed off World C3. Management is scared we might mess up the calibrations built into the glass sides."

Jordan nodded, then went on. "Point three. The technology here is more than just cutting edge, no pun intended. What you have from Officer Tan is that getting into the brain directly has medical possibilities. Is there a chance that military applications are really what this is all about? The ultimate ray gun. Get close enough and a trusted officer could be made to kill supreme leader."

"Or just mess with the programming itself," Fran said. "Assume this type of VR catches on and trusted officer likes playing with just a light-weight cap instead of a headset weighing maybe a pound or more. Get a game set up that assures virtual death becomes the real thing."

Jordan laughed. "Right. But you could only pull that off once, and I think that's what we've got here. Maybe getting the financials for No Limits will give us some answers."

Fran had already tried to do this. "That may not happen. I started searching for online links. The big issue is that No Limits is not a publicly traded company. No SEC reporting expected. Also nothing suggesting a Trump-style tell investors one thing and the tax guys another. It's privately owned, but there are separate divisions so that the playground is the only visible evidence of its existence."

"Like a shark's fin coming at you," Jordan said. He hummed the iconic music from Jaws. "Saw it on cable a few months back. Read up on how they made it. Too early for the kind of CGI we've been using for every comic book blockbuster in the last twenty years or so. That was also before credits got to be so damned long so that the apprentice assistants to the second assistant for something would see their names on the screen."

"You sound jealous."

"Got me there, Inspector. But, you know, there are some guys doing part-time work with the VR techs No Limits calls in to fix the glitches."

"They admit to glitches?"

"It's either that or the aliens are now among us with kindergarten stuff from another galaxy far, far away."

"And you're going to go snooping," Fran said.

"I'll do you a favor and keep the captain out if it."

"Please." Fran still had to give an account to Quine. The less she suggested she might be going rogue again, the more Quine might be willing to look the other way. For Christmas she had given him an autographed copy of Simon Oakland's headshot. Oakland had played Captain Bennet in Bullitt. It actually made Quine smile, just ever so slightly, but it was never a good idea to press her luck.

IX

Saturday Fran slept in, then spent the rest of the morning and a good part of the afternoon learning more about virtual gaming, or at least what was now public knowledge. What amazed her was the amount of money that had gone into setting up three-dimensional virtual worlds. An article from the beginning of the year in 2021 raved about how digital-property prices were hitting outrageous highs.

That had only been the beginning as every major brand wanted a virtual showcase and was willing to pay for it. So it stretched ad budgets. They did not want to be left out, and it would be even better if they had exclusive rights.

She wished Pop had lived to see all this. He had made it big with an import business, and he left enough to Fran and her brother that they could follow any career path they wanted. His one stipulation, not really needed for Fran but a good idea when it came to Brian, was that they had to be doing something that might help the world be a better place. She had gone to law school but never took the bar, doing a little of this and that until she decided on the SFPD.

Brian, not as tall as his sister but built like a tank, had made it into the pros as a linebacker. He had two unwearable Super Bowl rings that he let his son, Bryan Junior, try on every so often.

Junior, born with a serious heart condition, would never be out there running with a team. He was lucky still to be alive, but he made up with his mind what he could not accomplish with his body. He had been his aunt's tutor on the new language of block chains and crypto currency. He had advised his dad to get in early on Bitcoin, then get out just in time. Both father and son had demanded Fran forget about loans and mortgages. Get what she wanted and pay them back when she chose to.

A few smart investments of her own and she had done just that. She had gone to Hastings because she wanted to understand the system, especially how it had failed those who had not born white as well as many who had. She had not gone on to the bar exam because she did not want the system to take her over

Her secret film hero was Robert Duvall's consigliere in the Godfather films. In real life would she have worked for the Mafia? Hardly, but then gangs in California had no code of honor and even on the East Coast with characters like Whitey Bolger, playing both sides against the middle as crime boss and FBI informant, she would have felt she had sold her soul for nothing.

So now she was the system, "the man" for anyone who did not know her better. The one thing that got to her was watching a system meant to promote justice doing just the opposite. She always tried to do something about it when she could.

There were once important figures in San Francisco, including a few from SFPD, who had lots of time in one or another penitentiary to reflect on their sins as well as who called them out. That meant she better watch her back at all times, which is why she was glad Quine was one of the good guys. She was betting her life on it.

Bryan Junior had some info on No Limits that might help her. The money man was a really unpleasant dude named Baxter John Waterson. He had been born into a family that could trace its paternal lineage back to the original Knights of the White Camellia in Louisiana. His great-grandfather had been close to KWC's founder, Alcibiades DeBlanc, a former Confederate General who insisted on a paramilitary response to any effort to extend rights to Africans that they had not possessed before the Civil War and Lincoln's illegal declaration of emancipation.

The original group had faded away early in the twentieth century only to be revived during the civil rights struggles of the 1960s. Waterson's daddy had been a proud contributor to the group and the son, wealthy from early heavy investments in Microsoft, Apple, and Google, would easily have had a proper positioning in one magazine's list of billionaires. Unlike Trump, whom he had supported quite generously, he deplored ostentation of any kind. The only clue to what he wanted was his slogan: "White only, now and always."

The death of Jaime Morales now took on a new significance. It might have nothing to do with advancing No Limits as a business, everything with supporting white supremacy.

Fran thanked her nephew, then sent back to her research. Maybe now she had answered the question of why Jaime Morales had been killed, but she was no closer to how it was done.

X

Monday was a chance to start their investigation of the O'Farrell playground death with a new focus. Fran was grateful that Quine, who knew how to pull strings, had persuaded the key folks in local media to withhold any info on what happened at the site of the old O'Farrell theater. There was just a rumor that some college kid had been drinking too much and had to be taken to a hospital. No one had seen the gurney with a sheet covering Jaime's face, and Reed Ryder kept his mouth shut. He was not about to risk anyone taking a second or third look at where he fit in.

Arturo was getting through what might best be called PTSD with rotating counselors. The one thing that would still have to be done was to notify his folks, who were Mexican nationals. They had been away celebrating their silver anniversary with a trip to Hawaii and a leisurely cruise back to Ensenada. This gave everyone a chance to hold off planning a funeral.

The medical examiner had come back with what had been

learned in the autopsy. There was a puncture at the base of the boy's neck. It had reached through to his jugular vein.

Jaime's real death was not entirely simultaneous with his avatar's virtual one. By now the monitor had provided the evidence needed to establish that the virtual slaying had occurred at least thirty seconds before Jaime collapsed and fell out of his chair. Good news for the playground management. Not such good news for Arturo Morales, but Fran was not about to go with moving him to a jail cell.

What she had learned through her nephew's sleuthing only intensified her feeling that everything had been rigged for Jaime Morales to die where he did.

Meeting later in the day with Jordan Tran, Fran learned just how ground-breaking was the technology in use by No Limits. The night before Jordan had taken Amy on a pretend double date with Don Singh and Don's fiancée. She now said everyone should call her Ana, since she did not want to be confused with the famous writer, Amy Tan.

Jordan had met Don in a postgraduate workshop dealing with how to have a gamer seemingly experience physical movement without leaving his chair. One idea being kicked around was bypassing the five senses to manipulate the brain directly from the inside. Some experiments suggested this could be done.

"You remember," Don said, "how we compared ourselves with

the scientists working on the Manhattan Project. They saw how in theory compressing a uranium core could set off an explosion converting mass into energy. The job was to see how they could make it happen.

"Disregard that doing so contradicted the classic rule since Newton that they were just different realities, the way we think now of the dreams in our skulls and the sensory world outside our skulls. If we go with the parallel here, whoever wins the arms race with VR will dominate the future of gaming as long as there aren't leaks like they had with Julius and Ethel."

"But that's what No Limits seems to have done," Jordan said. "Instead of consoles the walls of a pod transmit to a game cap and then right into the player's brain while he sits comfortably in his chair. Think about the motive for any competitor to get close enough to see how that's done."

"If I were any of the other playground start-ups I'd sell my kids for that info," Don remarked. At that, Lorna, the intended mother of his kids, punched his arm. It was not a playful thing. She had seen a side of these VR guys that scared her.

Ana tried to ease the sudden tension. "We don't have to worry, guys. VR might have a new way of having a virtual experience, but we're still in control when it comes to what we're going to do."

"That's not what I hear," Don said. "There's a guy I talked to who thinks No Limits has a way of managing our hormones. Make you happy if they want, make you sad, make you mad enough to kill somebody. There's a rumor that something like that happened New Year's Eve. Someone managed to see them wheeling out a corpse. No word on the news, though. It's as though No Limits has bribed the police and everyone else to shut up."

Jordan started to say something, but this time Ana stopped him by deliberately knocking over his drink. He got the hint.

"Good thing you did," Fran said after getting his report. "But we need to see what killing a college kid is supposed to prove apart from showing it can be done. Why make it seem like a remake of what happened with the Mitchell brothers?"

"Maybe it's deliberate that the kids used here are Mexicans. Just less entitled to life, liberty and so on. You've found out that Waterson is the money man and also that he is one determined bigot.

"No," Fran replied. "I don't think it's because a Mexican life means less to Waterson. There's something else he's got in mind."

"Good luck guessing."

"Why guess when maybe I can have the man tell me himself?"

XI

January 6, 2000 had been either a day of infamy rivaling Pearl Harbor and the attack on the Twin Towers, or a day of glory as true patriots rallied to challenge a stolen election. Anniversaries were a time for one side to denounce the other, and in 2024 there was even a more apparent effort to rewrite its history in essentially racial terms: America was meant to be a white Christian nation with a restricted right to vote, a republic but by no means a democracy with the poor and the uneducated having an equal say in its management.

Fran Martinet had never seen herself required to support her Black sisters in each and every new cause. In this way she was like so many Black Americans, including one of it presidents, whose ancestors had neither been slaves nor second-class citizens living under Jim Crow. She had been called an Aunt Jemima on many occasions when she refused to go along with demands to display a greater degree of solidarity. Her answer had often been to pass on a copy of essays by Zora Neale Hurston, a writer she very much admired.

Proposals might be well-intentioned but it made no sense to ignore the probability of unintended consequences. Absurd proposals that would not allow young looters, burglars, car jackers, or muggers to be prosecuted as criminals were among the realities she found unacceptable. Granted, it was an effort to treat Black youngsters from the hood the same way as the white teens who never spent a full day behind bars. The result in San Francisco had been to end Market Street as a place to go shopping, and Fran had liked to shop.

Her own way of handling things as a cop had been to take a personal interest in the kids she met. She might or might not use paperwork. Her preference was to get to know a family, assuming there was one. When there was nothing stable at home she would call in a few favors to give a kid a chance to straighten out. It did not always work out, but then Officer Martinet might let quite different acquaintances take over.

Crime, especially organized crime, was just a reality in any society large enough to have parallel structures. Japan with its ritualized Yakuza subculture was an example of fairly harmonious balance between the legitimate and the criminal. So was Las Vegas after the war and Atlantic City during prohibition. Marlon Brando in *The Godfather* and James Gandolfini in *The Sopranos* portrayed ruthless mobsters with a thin veneer of respectability that might even deceive their own children.

Pop, who succeeded in the import business in part because he knew whom to pay off the books, had made sure Fran got to know the right people for particular needs. He had been a charming but potentially dangerous man who taught Fran how to handle herself both physically and mentally.

"Friends" in Chinatown taught her how to fight as though her life depended on it.

Exiles from around the world help her develop moderate conversational skills in Chinese (Mandarin as well as a bit of the distinct dialects of Hong Kong and Shanghai), French, and Russian. She had been an apt student. Her aural memory, which normally slows down markedly with puberty, was extraordinary while her skills at facial recognition had actually improved.

The one person she felt closest to beyond her own family was known simply as Uncle Sam. He was a short, wizened Eurasian with no other admission about what ethnicities were involved. His age was a mystery as well. Some families in Little Russia, an area in the Richmond off Geary, swore he had been the fixer who arranged the forged documents that got them out of Shanghai just before Tojo's murderous assault. Fran suspected there was a father to son transference of identities, much like the way the Voodoo priestess Marie LaVeau was thought to have lived on within her daughter in nineteenth century New Orleans.

Pop had sworn by the man, entrusting Fran to his tutelage since Bryan could only think of football. Sam had encouraged her law studies at Hastings, suggesting that even if she never took her bar exam, she would have some very good friends who did.

Over the years since she had graduated she came to know more about both California politics in general and Bay Area conspiracies in particular than even Bob Raskin, the columnist who supposedly knew everything and did not hesitate it to share it with his readers in the San Francisco Chronicle. Several times, when very crooked prominent citizens found themselves Fran's target, her leaks to Raskin had sealed their fate.

In her fast rise from walking a beat to being a detective, Fran Martinet had made connections that might help some crooks while damning others. Much seemed to depend on whether they were Uncle Sam's idea of good crooks. Raskin often served as an intermediary.

Bax Waterson had never made Sam's list, and the reporter thoroughly relished the idea of bringing him down. Accordingly, he made sure invitations were sent out that invited Inspector Mary Frances Martinet to sit at the same table with Waterson on January 6, Patriot Day for the true believers convinced that, had Mr. Trump won the 2020 election, the Confederacy would rise again.

XII

Fran did vary her wardrobe for the occasion. Department rules for dress had only grudgingly been altered for female or non-binary officers, primarily to allow for earrings. The latest rules had allowed for jackets that, except for color, resembled those designed for the Space Force uniforms—high-collar dark blue jackets and slacks, an angular row of buttons, medals or ribbons on the right breast of the jacket.

For functions such as the Patriots Dinner she did not need to be carrying a sidearm or anything else that might be needed for an arrest. She did, however, have one of her favorite knives in a sheath above her right ankle. She also made sure to wear her gold medal of valor. Headwear was optional, so she her kept Jada Pinkett look.

The dinner was at one of the new luxury hotels built to replace an office building on Market Street. The promoters may not have expected Mary Frances Martinet to look like she did, but the attendants, all Asian, greeted her with special enthusiasm. She had skipped the cocktail reception, so she was one of the last to be seated. The room suddenly hushed as other guests noticed her, some with slightly audible gasps as she was seated next to Mr. Waterson, the guest of honor. Baxter himself stood to greet her, as did the others in his party with more obvious reluctance.

"Inspector, I am happy that you were able to make it. Mr. Raskin did not exaggerate when he has referred to you as Black, big, bald, and beautiful. I would like to think we have one of those characteristics in common." He pointed to his head as he said this.

Fran could not help smiling. Uncle Sam had briefed her well. He had compared the man to the serpent in the garden, wisest of the creatures in Eden and certainly charming enough to lure any woman to that first bite of the apple.

"I see that chivalry lives on, Mr. Waterson."

"Please, even if we are not yet old friends, do call me Bax. May I call you Fran?"

She nodded and sat down as he held the chair for her. His troop then sat down as well, still hesitant about what they should say in turn. Committed patriots all, they were comfortable with Black females only when they were supine and accommodating. The slang was that they would be playing Tom Jefferson, not otherwise admired in his failure to acknowledge that religion should always be a major consideration in government actions. It was obvious that race would always be primary.

Waterson picked up the slack by maintaining a conversation about how San Francisco weather had changed since he was a young man. Fisherman's Wharf had long since been abandoned and playful seals lounged along the decks of the Embarcadero, often enough blocking the path of the renovated streetcars that still ran from Market Street out to Van Ness.

The dinner itself was superb. Fran and Waterson both appreciated culinary excellence, and they compared notes on their favorite restaurants. Fran's had been a Thai restaurant on Geary, Waterson's a classic steak house on Van Ness. Again the others at the table decided it would be better to say nothing. One reason might have been that they had not yet graduated to anything more sophisticated than hamburgers at McD's.

There was to be time at the end for coffee and a cordial before the night's ceremonies began, typically with a chaplain invoking the sainted martyrs of the Capitol protests to bless this evening's activities. Waterson took Fran by the arm and led her to a small conference room off the main hall.

Once inside, he apologized for not letting her remain to watch the Patriot ceremonies. "I am sure you have something of a reason to be here this evening. And I suppose it concerns one of my more interesting business ventures."

"It does, and what I am trying to understand is who in your C-suite wants to have it fail."

Waterson seemed genuinely puzzled. Apparently, he had not yet been informed of how a young Cal student had not just experienced a virtual death but a very real one.

Fran had the good poker player's ability to recognize tells. No, he did not know—at least this evening—that something had gone very wrong with one of his enterprises. Perhaps the No Limits people had limits about what they wanted their principal and—as far as she knew the only—investor to know. It was practically a rule with the military, as the American public had learned about Vietnam and Afghanistan and might still learn about Africa.

He listened intently as Fran ran through what happened and what she had come to suspect.

"And you saw me as a person of interest in some way because of my avowed support of white supremacy. Killing off a Mexican was not really much more than swatting a mosquito."

"In a nutshell."

"Fran, then you do not really understand my position. For instance, I have only the highest respect for any individual who achieves excellence regardless of race. I know enough about you to resent how the group at my table failed to show you the same courtesy as I did. Moreover, I do not share the Aryan premise of superior genes, something which Mr. Trump accepted.

It is simply that in a society that does not start off fully integrated a contest for superior position is destructive. It is usually an accident of history how color has played such a role, and the resolution I find most interesting is how the same group, those we just call Indo-Europeans today, forcibly taking over territory in Europe or America, also took over India without resorting to either slavery or genocide. They instituted a caste system and justified it with the mythology of rebirth.

"Had the advanced cultures in Africa been at all interested in expansion and used a similar tactic, we might well be talking about black supremacy. It almost happened in Haiti, and you have a proud heritage. Your father, for instance, was someone who might well have been the billionaire, and I would have been hoping for crumbs from his table."

Fran was momentarily at a loss for words. More than once she had heard Pop talk much the same way as Waterson did.

"You will have my full cooperation in determining just what did happen to the young man who died. Also, I will see about providing assistance to his brother. But I think you may be mistaken about why someone went to the considerable effort to have the brothers at the No Limits Club. I tend to think you are quite correct that at least one of them was an intended target, but that it was meant to remind anyone of the Mitchell brothers is just a coincidence."

"And could there be a reason to make it look like a problem with this new technology itself?"

"Fran, perhaps the opposite in some way. Regardless, I can certainly arrange for you to experience the game that the brothers themselves were involved in. This may prove of benefit to both of us."

XIII

It had now been a week since Jaime Morales was killed. Early Thursday she asked Jordan Tran to go with her to the still closed No Limits Club. Waterson had been good to his word. A small corps of the team responsible for the O'Farrell Street playground were ready to be of assistance. They understood that the inspector and her companion were to have the opportunity to experience the script for "Escaping Jack the Ripper."

"In exactly the same chairs," Fran demanded.

One of the team—Brad, according to the ID on his shirt— immediately volunteered that the chair the deceased player had been using was now down in the room for damaged equipment. Jaime's blood had apparently damaged some of the wiring.

Jordan picked up on this immediately. "Brad, what kind of wiring was in the chair? I thought it was just the cap that had anything electronic."

Brad wanted to be helpful. "Well, the game cap feeds stimuli to the same neural synapses that our eyes and ears do, but for a full sensory experience you need the skin's own receptors for touch and pain. This is how when your avatar picks up an object you actually feel its weight and texture as though it is your own hand holding it."

"And how much pain is possible?" Fran asked.

"Well," Brad said, "it is obviously attenuated. In the script you can step through fire or be tossed into boiling water, but you really are not feeling burned or scalded. This is why we can offer superhero adventures far more exciting than other VR offerings. The game cap does only part of this. The rest is an adaptation of the Tesla suits that came out a few years back to get full-body sensory experiences. In looks they resemble the Kevlar vests you guys all enjoy wearing, especially in hot weather. They worked by having connections with your upper torso and feeding into the brain with a connection at the nape of your neck.

"Of course, those first jackets coast twenty grand apiece. Our techs figured how to use a nice reclining chair to work the same way at half the cost. When you are immersed in the game, spring action allows its tip to connect with the autonomic ganglia that relay impulses back and forth throughout your body."

Fran saw immediately what could have happened. Replace the intended connector with a needle-like object and intensify the strength of the spring. The question would be timing.

Chances were that whatever had been in that chair had already been disposed of. All that was left was to sit through what Jaime and Arturo sat through. They were seated in World C4, presumably no different from World C3 as it was a week before.

The VR caps were not at all uncomfortable. Fran and Jordan were advised that for the best experience they should still close their eyes even though the pod itself would be dark. They were asked to accept the selected script and mentally consented.

Jordan, who spent much of his workday with the equipment for both AR and VR, marveled at the material in the cap. It stretched easily enough for different head sizes but remained firm. The amount of hair that it covered did not seem to matter.

Fran was aware of the very slight pressure on her neck from whatever it was at the top of the chair. There was no reason to think it had been tampered with, but she now wished she had worn one of her sweaters with a high collar. Just in case.

Fran had never been interested in VR games, so for her it was a new and rather disturbing experience. Her presence on the streets of London was through a female avatar armed with a dagger. She was able to look at her limbs through the avatar's eye, and thanks to the chair itself she could feel the touch of one hand on the other. So far, the only difference between what she could see around her and an old IMAX movie with throwaway 3D glasses was that she was obviously in control of where she was walking and what she was doing as the script played on.

The original excitement with VR games had peaked early in the decade for several reasons. One was the limited content of material. Another was a tendency to induce motion sickness, and already Fran was trying to ward off a tendency to walk as though she had been hitting the bottle. What she did find exciting was that she had company as she walked. Since there were only two players, all other avatars were directed just by the script. What she was supposed to look out for would be Jack the Ripper leaping from a darkened alley. He might be dressed as any of the other figures she saw, but the difference would be in how he acted.

That happened about five minutes into the session. Jack was suddenly there behind her, almost close enough to strike. Other figures were running in panic, and presumably she was supposed to do the same. Fran just looked for a moment. This was just like the self-defense classes she had taken as a rookie. After the first few Fran had been excused.

Thanks to Pop, she had been trained in a mix of techniques that were not meant for typical martial arts contests in that their goal was not to subdue but actually kill an opponent. She reacted just as though this was another such drill, only Jack lacked the protective gear a pretend attacker would have had on. He lost his virtual head, and not just as a figure of speech.

Lights had gone on and during actual business hours the floor attendant would have been summoned from his office a story below.

"Ah, Fran, why did you have to do that?" Jordan asked. "I was just trying to see how the No Limits wizards adjusted for rotation, and then I looked over and you're going all Bruce Lee."

Brad came back into the cubicle. "That was a first," he said, "and I don't know whether to laugh or cry."

XIV

The team was back in the office for debriefing.

Brad was explaining why Fran's actions during the game had short-circuited the script. "For any of our games to be fully interactive we need to get input from a player's brain. The fact that in the game you appear to be walking or running along a street is the most obvious example. What players used to do with a handheld controller can now be done, quite literally, just by thinking about it.

"It is just a matter of improving the technology that got started in the last decade. We've taken this a few steps forward with our game caps accessing the largest organ in the human body, the skin itself.

"Inspector, your actions in the game exceeded the parameters of the chips embedded in the pod's windows. Even with just your mind you acted with at least twice as much speed and force as the receptors were designed to accommodate."

Fran saw that Jordan, nodding appreciatively, appeared to

understand what Brad was talking about. She might be an expert in a number of areas traditionally studied by police officers, but electronic wizardry was not one of them.

"So the game ended, and you came in," she said.

"The game ended, but there is a short gap in your memory. It's from a signal that approximates what happens to a footballer when he's been hit in the head and concussed, but there is no damage at all to the brain. It is strictly a security measure."

"What kind of security?

"There are things happening once an abnormal event takes place in a script. One of them is just coding that will allow our programmers to isolate whether the event has otherwise affected the mother script being streamed. We really do not want to have our clients distracted by it. And, obviously, we do not want the competition to know too much about any internal issues. All our stuff is just beta but we want to look better."

Brad smiled at his pun. Jordan winced appropriately. Fran remained lost in her own thoughts.

The death of Jaime Morales had seemed like one of those locked-room mysteries that mystery authors like to invent. If she assumed Brad had not been outside the pod all along, he had been alerted and made it in before either she or her partner were even aware that the game had stopped. Maybe she did not have to imagine making the neck rest a weapon.

"Who else in your team was on board a week back?"

"New Year's Eve? That was Victor Chavez. He was our promotions manager."

"Would that mean he had something to do with the lottery that got the Morales brothers here?"

"He had everything to do with it. He wanted to make things more personal for the winners. The rest of us in management went home early, but he wanted to be here for meet and greet."

"Was there anything maybe out of the ordinary about him that day?"

"Just really excited. Well, a couple of times he said something about an eye for an eye."

XV

Quine reviewed her report, then leaned back for a minute to decide just how to handle it.

"Fran, how much do you know about the Mexican cartels? Apart from the newspapers, that is."

"Probably not as much as I should. Bosses die or go to prison, underlings fight each other like hyenas after a kill."

"Well, let's bring you up to date about the action around the border with Texas. Nuevo Laredo has always been a hell hole, but of the minor incidents—measured by how long anyone mentioned it on TV—one that stood out last year happened when a breakaway group headed by Rodolfo Anguiano attacked a three-car caravan on its way to a wedding. The victims were innocent civilians, several of them from Texas and California. Most of them shared the same last name: Chavez. With me so far?"

"And this connects somehow with Victor Chavez of No Limits."

"Who also used to be known as Major Victor Chavez USMC, delegated to work with various companies involved in developing training materials for the military. He resigned his commission shortly after the Nuevo Laredo massacre, then on the basis of his background managed to get a position with No Limits."

That did not quite answer why he would go out of his way to target Jaime Morales. This was the obvious question, and Quine was ready to answer it.

"We got some info from Cal about Arturo. The brothers' full surname reflects the Hispanic tradition of citing mom as well as dad. Most often one or the other gets dropped for everyday use."

Fran felt a chill as the pieces began to fall into place.

"Jaime's full last name is Morales-Anguiano," he said. "An eye for an eye. One down, more to go. Remember that a lot of things, especially a proper funeral, had to be put on hold because the parents were celebrating their anniversary with a cruise. Now here's the part you are not going to like at all. Your guy from No Limits called a while back. Chavez handed in his resignation on Monday, said he's got a new gig working for Skyline Cruises. He was going to meet one of their ships in Honolulu and help install new VR games."

The next bit of info was that other agencies had taken an interest in the case, particularly the Air Force itself. Victor Chavez had access to more classified material than he was entitled to.

"Apparently," Quine explained, "he was shopping stuff on the military applications of VR. Not the training materials, understand, but combat applications."

"That could be scary," Fran said.

"Agreed. That's why I'm letting the Air Force have you for a while. Lieutenant Colonel Bill Mowrey will be flying on to Honolulu, and he specifically asked for you to go with him. Two birds with one stone, and all that. You might be able to come back with a way we can get this guy for the Morales murder."

Fran found it difficult to keep a straight face.

Quine nodded. "All right, I know that you two had a thing going a few years ago. What you do on your downtime is none of my business. Just nail this sucker."

"Yes, sir," she agreed. Now it was Big Bad Wolf teaming up again with Lamb Chop the Cop. This could be fun, as long as Chavez did not have too many surprises waiting for them.

XVI

"Lamb chop?" Jordan Tran asked, trying hard not to laugh.

Fran nodded. "So it's a code name. Get over it. I need you and Ana to pump the No Limits team for more about how wireless transmission works inside their pods. Chavez got a job with them, but since he wasn't a techie it had to be more than just finding a weird way to murder Jaime Morales. He already had a lot of stolen material ready to go to the highest bidder, but we don't know much else. I think he was looking for more."

"I take it that you don't think Waterson is involved."

"No, I don't. He saw this as an interesting investment, and the only evidence that it fits his mindset otherwise is what Arturo has told us about some of the first games they played. They were both racist and sadistic. The only possible justification might be that a virtual experience of what it might feel like to be on the receiving end of, say, a slave beating would make you more 'woke' somehow."

"That's a stretch," Jordan said.

"Agreed.   So let's just keep with the idea that No Limits developed edgy experiences that two or more clients could share without being in physical contact.   What I think might have been something worth stealing is how they could induce temporary amnesia with their electronic beanies if something goes wrong with the script."

Jordan had a suggestion.   "One thing we might do is ask for the monitor records that include games ending prematurely.   Keep in mind they record events in a proprietary digital shorthand, and there has to be a code in there that triggers the amnesia."

"Not much help for us if we ever wanted to go to a DA," Fran commented.   "Too Looney Tunes."

Jordan stared at her.   "What's Looney Tunes?"

"Ah, you poor youngsters.   Kids used to watch these great animated cartoons with characters like Porky Pig and Bugs Bunny and Elmer Fudd."

"Like Manga?"

"Not really.   Came a time not that long back when it became a very bad thing to laugh at Porky Pig and Elmer Fudd because they stuttered."

"So Looney Tunes means something inappropriate?"

"No, it means something silly. Going to a DA with what we know so far means getting laughed at."

Jordan sighed. "Okay, Lamb Chop, I'll see what we can find out for you."

XVII

Fran took a commercial redeye to Honolulu. She skipped the welcoming flower necklace, was picked up in a military jeep for a quick ride to the Air Force base at Hickam Field, and met up with Bill Mowrey in a room he had commandeered for their mission.

"Inspector Martinet, I presume."

They both laughed. It had been a long while since they had worked together. Back then there had been time for romantic R & R when their mission was accomplished, but neither expected nor wanted a lasting relationship. This time they'd have to see how much of a spark was left, but for the next few days they had to be all business. But they still were on a first-name basis.

"Fran, you went through one of these No Limits simulations. How was it?"

"From their perspective it was a disaster. It seems I over-reacted to someone trying to kill me. Their script could not handle my avatar decapitating their avatar for Jack the Ripper."

"Too bad for them," Bill said. "We both got trained to do what we have to. What weapon did you use in the simulation?"

"Just my hand flat-out. You know the karate move, slice at the throat. Well, a virtual action is supposed to exaggerate what's happening when you move in real life, or in this case just think about moving in a certain way."

"So a virtual killing is less work than a real one," Bill commented. "Maybe that should reduce the homicide rate. So what happened then?"

"They handle something like that by having you go blank for a couple of minutes or more. We think this is what gave Chavez a chance to murder the kid."

"And how do you know that's what happened?"

"Apparently, the point is that we don't. I suppose that if you were getting a complete biometric read-out it might show somehow."

Bill had been jotting down notes as they talked. "That means two things with obvious implications for national security. One is that the No Limits geniuses have figured a way to have a machine-brain interface with just the walls around you taking the place of a console. The second is that part of the interface is the ability to mess with your sense of time.

"You know already that once the Defense Department started taking UFO reports seriously, the easiest explanation was that what Navy pilots said they saw would be like shining a laser at the ceiling in a dark room. It can be like the slow and steady movement of an actual object, or it can be jumping all over the place like a virtual object. The problem was we did not have the technology to create such phenomena, and we were concerned about potential enemies that might."

"How much can we assume Chavez knew before he signed on with No Limits?" Fran asked.

"A lot might be that he had bits and pieces but no way to put them together, especially since he was not a gamer himself. And we do not know any contacts he may have had with potential buyers."

"Next question. If he's signed on to the cruise ship as their VR entertainment guy, how does this fit in with his eye-for-an-eye mission with the Anguiano parents? He can't pull the same stunt as we think he did with the boy."

"That's what we're going to find out. The ship left port yesterday. We've been in touch with the captain, and he's expecting us onboard at about one tomorrow morning.

"Can we trust him not to alert our targets?" Fran asked.

"Hard to say," Bill replied. "It doesn't matter that much anyway. We fly out in a Marine hovercraft a bit before midnight, then go down a rope ladder to the rear deck. Any passengers staying up past their bedtime will have been ordered off. We go to our cabins, get some sleep, then act like we've been on the ship all along.

"That means you go shopping at government expense today for something fancy, but I'll be wearing my best ugly Hawaiian outfit. We stay separate as much as possible. Chavez has never seen you and shouldn't know anything about you, so you can play the dumb passenger who's just getting over being seasick and see whether he finds you cute enough to chat up."

Fran had never worked in disguise. In San Francisco that would have been impossible, and the last time she had worked with Bill Mowrey was over in Oakland. He had been the undercover agent that time. It was right after she had made the rank of inspector, and Quine had asked her to help the Air Force track down a couple of rogue pilots. Bill got made, and she had to lead a team to rescue him.

"Cute enough," she said. "I'll be really cute if that's what it takes. You might be sorry, Bill. I might even find the man of my dreams."

"Well, you can tone it down a bit at that," he answered.

Yes, she realized, that man was already there, but they both knew why it couldn't work. At least not yet.

XVIII

Other passengers on the cruise had no way of knowing that the handsome couple sitting at the captain's table were celebrities for the wrong reason. Rodolfo and Imelda Anguiano were the public face of the Rosa Negra cartel as it began moving from drugs to a more contemporary merchandise. The emblem of a black rose now appeared on ads in leading business journals along with those recruiting for old-fashioned intelligence agencies such as the CIA and MI 6.

They traded in what were being called taffies because of their resemblance to the Turkish Taffy candies where you could break off a piece at a time. This itself was an instance of full stack developments, controlling both what a user saw on a screen and what went on for that to happen.

The Japanese, always ahead of the curve when it came to a new hot technology, had encouraged the few remaining Yakusa leaders to coordinate with the criminal empires of both allies and rivals ("enemies" was such an unhelpful word) to note and then appropriate by any means necessary new ways if manipulating how ordinary citizens understood whatever one might mean by the word "reality." Anything significant was given a K rating (in tribute to the actor Keanu Reeves).

The Israelis, once in trouble for software that allowed governments to monitor private conversations, usually got high K ratings, but the Mexican government was close behind. On the principle that it you can't beat them then join them the cartels were being co-opted to serve government interests. Breakdowns were rare, but one had happened when Rosa Negra gunmen ambushed cars carrying what were thought to be the family of another, somewhat uncooperative cartel. It was flagged as a friendly fire incident.

Unfortunately, they had not counted on one of their better military informants belonging to that family. Victor Chavez had lost both his oldest son and his mother, and he was a firm believer in the ancient code of an eye for an eye.

Rodolfo succeeded where many of his predecessors failed because he was not in the least sentimental. Imelda had not yet been told that one of her boys was dead, somehow murdered by Chavez. He understood that in the symmetry of things he must allow himself to become a widower.

One potential disruption was the presence of an American couple who also had an interest in Chavez. The man, an Air Force officer intent on interfering with the digital merchandise Chavez was selling, would be the victim of a tragic accident. The woman, however, was not to be harmed. This was a personal request from one of his American associates, and it was not a good idea to cross Baxter Waterson.

What he had not counted on was that one of the men in his party wanted to get away from his partner's snoring. The man had checked the ship's manifest and discovered there was an empty room on the third deck. Taking a master code key he went up to the room and let himself in. He was barely inside when he realized someone else had beat him to it.

Fran Martinet had been trying to get some sleep after the flight from Hickam. She was not in a good mood, especially since she had almost been dropped into the water as the rope ladder swung across the rear deck. Bill Mowrey, already on the deck, had grabbed her just in time.

One thing she always did in a strange room was put her boots against the door. She had almost dropped off when she heard the boots being shoved aside as the door opened. It had made her leap from the bed and pin the intruder against the wall. The man made the mistake of reaching for the gun at his waist. It clattered to the floor with its owner falling on top of it as Fran hit him with a powerful blow to the side of his head. He was out for the count.

XIX

Bill had been thinking about sleep in his room on the next deck above when Fran reached him on the ship intercom. By the time he reached her room the intruder was regaining consciousness but seemed to have no idea of what had just happened. He looked from Bill to Fran, both taller than he was by at least ten inches and perhaps the same weight but with muscle where he had fat. The key difference alerting him that something must have gone very wrong was that the woman was holding his somewhat antique Browning Hi-Power.

"Who told you to come to this room?" Bill asked in a tone that indicated an evasive answer would not be acceptable. The man was definitely puzzled.

Fran repeated the question in Spanish. He began jabbering about his snoring roommate and how he had gone to the bridge to see if he could get an empty room. This was just a terrible mistake and he was very sorry.

"¿Por que la arma?"

"Para proteger la dama, Señora Morales."

"He has a gun to protect Mrs. Morales," Fran said.

"That I could understand, even with just my high school D, but he's way out of shape for a bodyguard. See if the thing is even loaded."

Fran checked. "It is, but this rod hasn't been cleaned in years. He'd be safer throwing it at someone"

She began interrogating him more carefully. His name was Paco Morales, and Imelda was his aunt. If her husband could travel with highly trained bodyguards, at least she could treat her favorite nephew to a holiday on the ocean. The other guys liked him, even tried to get him in shape. They had nicknamed him Gordito, the little fat guy.

It was the perfect opportunity to learn more about the less than happy couple celebrating their anniversary. Rodolfo Anguiano had taken an interest in an actress starring in a major telenovela, and he had agreed to the cruise as a peace offering when Imelda had learned about it. So far she had kept to herself. Paco said she wanted to make new friends.

A perfect opportunity. Fran had just one more question. How well was she handling her son's death? Paco's shock seemed very real. He had liked his cousins very much. She would not have come on this cruise had she known this. Yes, now he must make sure Fran would meet his aunt. Imelda would very much want to know what had happened from the very police officer investigating Jaime's murder.

XX

Paco was ordered back to his original room. He was to say nothing about the *agentes de policía americanos* to his bodyguard buddies, but as soon as possible he would tell his aunt that she should make friends with a very tall Black woman who would be reading a book at breakfast. Yes, Imelda spoke English, and she was also an American citizen since she had been born in Nogales, Arizona. No, he would just say that Fran was a reporter who would like to interview her.

Bill and Fran did their best to get a few hours' sleep. They would meet up later in the morning.

At eight Fran had taken a table set for two in the dining area. She sipped at her coffee while pretending to read from one of the books available to passengers.

It took about twenty minutes before a petite woman dressed in a blue sun dress asked in English whether she might join her, explaining that Paco had told her about a reporter hoping for an interview.

They shook hands and Imelda sat down. "Why really did you want to meet me?"

Fran shook her head. "I guess I don't really look much like a reporter, do I?"

Imelda smiled. "I would guess it has something to do with my husband."

"Not directly. It's about your son Jaime."

"Then something has happened to him. My birthday was five days ago while we were still in Hawaii. My sons always call."

Fran liked to think she had a sixth sense when it came to people, especially women. Despite her appearance, Jaime's mother was made of steel. All right, let her know the situation.

Imelda listened, then asked the one question that mattered at the moment.

"Is my husband planning to kill me?"

"More likely he is simply accepting that Chavez will somehow make an accident happen, one that also may be to his advantage."

Imelda was silent for a minute. "I am not surprised. It is why I asked to have Francisco come with me. My sister's son is very clever. Making himself something of a mascot for Rodolfo's bodyguards lets him pick up useful information. Also, he has a very old gun that was a family souvenir. It has been fixed so that you cannot actually pull the trigger, but he does not know that. I think the other men do know but play along."

"Well, one thing I would recommend," Fran said, "is not to take part in any of the VR games that may be set up. This is what we think Chavez used in San Francisco."

"I would not do that anyway," Imelda advised her. "I have a pacemaker and, even though it is shielded, I try to avoid most of these newer technologies. But now I must ask this. I am not a forgiving person, whatever the Gospels may say. Can you not just kill this evil man now?"

Fran placed her hands over Imelda's. There was no way she would tell her that, were it not for Bill, she would be quite happily arranging for Chavez to make a quick departure from the planet. The most she would admit is that she thought Chavez was already gambling with his life by being aboard. They would just have to wait and see how he played out his hand.

XXI

It was early afternoon in San Francisco when Jordan and Ana managed to reach Fran's cell. They had been with a special team investigating all aspects of how Jaime Morales had died. A few hours back they had finally returned to look at both the gaming chairs that had been in World C3.

Jaime's chair, in a downstairs area where it would be cleaned, seemed otherwise intact. In the pod the chair Arturo had been using appeared to have been tampered with. The cable for the mechanism that ended the game if someone got up from the chair had been cut. In moving the chair from its base on the floor Jordan found a small icepick with a blood-stained tip wedged under it.

"Fran, we hate to spoil your day, but we dusted for fingerprints, and you won't like what we found."

"You are going to tell me they were Arturo's."

"That's the story, but that doesn't mean he knows what

happened. Remember, the game should have stopped as soon as either brother got out of his chair. With the chair damaged we really don't know when he had that two-minute blackout. For all we know, he might have been fully aware of Chavez coming in, killing his brother but making sure Arturo's fingerprints were on the weapon, then tossing it under the chair. Then it all became a blank."

"And presumably he would not have known about the damaged cable," Fran said.

Ana joined in. "There's another possibility. If that game cap could induce amnesia, could it also induce a hypnotic trance?"

Fran did not like what she was hearing. She had never been persuaded about the reason cited for having any kind of memory gap. Brad had told her it was so that in the event of a breakdown in the script the client would not be subjected to random bits of coding that might themselves prove uncomfortable.

In the flight over from Hickam she had asked Bill about what he might already know. Granted, he said, the games were already disturbing because of their racist and sadistic content. Having a more direct input to the brain than had never been available without a microchip implant allowed for far more dangerous outcomes. It could become QAnon on steroids.

"The programmers for No Limits include ex-military, some with dishonorable discharges," Bill explained. "A few of these guys date back to 2020 and the attack on the Capitol. Chavez himself is strictly an intermediary. He managed to get a few taffies that, as far as I've been told, are the electronic equivalent of the biological weapons we're pledged to avoid."

Fran had required a five-minute seminar on the terminology, then she had asked just what they were supposed to accomplish by being on this cruise. How did he expect to stop the cartel from getting these programs?

"That's not the mission. I have some very special candy. We call it D & D, but that doesn't stand for Dungeons and Dragons. It means Detect and Destroy. The cruise itself is meant to be show and tell. If the new VR games fail to work as intended, Chavez will most likely be terminated."

Bill did not have to add the qualification, familiar from the days of the CIA working with informants in Vietnam, that he would be terminated with extreme prejudice.

XXII

Fran was definitely Imelda's new BFF. What's more, they actually did enjoy each other's company. Imelda did not go near the new VR pods, but she did like to gamble. She had never been properly initiated into the finer points of blackjack, so in the casino area they sat side by side and gradually Fran guided her to the point that she could play quite respectably on her own.

Ronaldo had come by and she introduced Fran to him as a friend from California. He greeted her as Inspector Martinet, inwardly seething at the immunity his far more important business partner from California had granted her.

She smiled at his greeting. Okay, the disguise, such as it was, was worthless, not that she had expected anything else. She decided to see what more Ronaldo really knew but above all how he knew it.

"I think we must have a friend in common," she said.

"Ah, Señor Waterson, un hombre muy intelligente. He

understands that cultural supremacy is not a matter of color, or else you would already have been among the unfortunate *desaparacidos* of my world."

"Soy demasiado grande para desaparecer facilmente," she replied. She was too big to disappear easily

Ronaldo had to agree. This woman, regardless of color, wasn't going to go away easily. Her partner was a quite different story. At least he hoped so.

XXIII

As they met up again, Bill thought it time to explain why his mission to intercept Victor Chavez had serious implications for national security. It might also explain just what had happened at the No Limits playground.

"Arturo Morales did act to kill his brother, but it could just as easily have gone the other way depending on who was in the tampered chair. But I'm pretty sure he was in no way really conscious of this."

Fran was well aware of the need-to-know rules that Lieutenant Colonel Mosely played by.

"One of the major issues," he explained, "is keeping civilian software designers from playing with possibilities just because they can. One of those possibilities was that brief time-out if something goes wrong with the script in a No Limits game. That was developed with a Space Force contract, but we were unable to prevent it escaping the reservation.

"A closely related possibility was parallel to what happens with hypnotic suggestion. The player is being told what to do without being aware of it. In San Francisco it involved leaving an ice pick with the drinks and snacks, then having Arturo pocket it at a break between games. His brother probably never saw him do it. Then at the proper moment Arturo does get out his chair, goes around the partition, and stabs Jaime."

"Why develop this kind of stuff?" Fran asked.

"Because the cybergeniuses of Russia, Israel, China, Japan and God knows where else would be working on this also. It's why we may have sworn off biochemical warfare but still must know what can be done, since it's a sure bet that having an ultimate weapon of mass destruction is every dictator's dream."

"And how did Chavez get involved?"

"He was being groomed for it. He nearly went off the rails when he learned what had happened to his own mother and brother, and this gave our mastermind the opportunity to test how well the apps worked as well as aim for a very big payday by using him to field test them, first in San Francisco, then right here on this ship."

"Who is the mastermind?" Fran asked.

"It's not Waterson, if that's what you were thinking," Bill said. "He backs interesting projects, but he's not Dr. No or any other character out of an old James Bond movie. And when I say 'mastermind' I don't mean to say it's just one individual, and it's not clear that those involved really have the big picture. My assigned mission has been to sabotage what's going on, which is the one and only reason I have been allowed my little D & D piece of software. Anything more than that is above my pay scale."

At this, he reached inside his shirt to pull off a thin rectangular plastic case. "Here's the taffy for what we're doing now."

He opened the case to remove a flat block of colored squares that locked into each other to form two rows, each four squares long. He slapped at the bottom row and it came apart easily.

"Just like the old candy I remember as a kid—a block of hard taffy that you had to hit against something to break off a piece to eat. It's a great example of stacking. Put this baby in one of your newer computer bays and you have a full set of interactive and immersive video games, none lasting more than an hour. The bottom row just happens to have my detect and destroy programs. I've already used them as I walked through the VR gaming stations.

"I'm expecting to be pretty well manhandled sometime soon, and Anguiano's goons will think they've got my secret weapon. What I want you to do is put it where they won't be looking."

Fran, like any female cop, knew what he meant.

"And what happens to you?"

"I suppose they'll not kill me right off. Instead, they'll toss me over to swim with the sharks. A terrible accident. There's a sub that's been tracking us, and I have an implanted chip for them to locate me. A bit longer and they'll surface to take over this ship. Just make sure you stay alive long enough yourself."

XXIV

Fran joined Imelda for lunch. Bill's sabotage was already creating a high degree of consternation among the truly addicted gamers. For Fran it brought back memories of the Superbowl a few years back when a beer commercial kept playing for the last thirty seconds of the game while the underdog team on the field made a miraculous comeback that would go down in sports history. The brewery found its products boycotted and soon went bankrupt.

The Anguiano party—the couple and their four supposed bodyguards—suddenly became the center of attention. About fifty passengers had traveled to Hawaii from both Europe and Asia to pay an outrageously high fare to be on this cruise. The cartel had let it be known in the right circles that the VR gaming available would include pirated material that had the potential to redefine international relations.

Out of the four hundred or so passengers, close to half had

already experienced something of the total immersion these new VR games made possible. Earlier games had essentially been about conquering aliens or fantastic creatures. These were either about subjugating fellow humans or escaping subjugation. This was not at all like the almost comical metaverses they were used to. Not everyone was a fan, but there was a disturbing difference with those who were. Impatience and belligerence were a bad combination.

Fran made sure Imelda got back to her cabin, then hurried to get someplace relatively secure on deck.

Until a short while before, Bill had a been just another tall, well-built brother talking football. Then the captain had pointed him out and he was surrounded by some of the irate players. Ronaldo had joined them along with a man that she recognized as Victor Chavez. The action seemed to be going just as Bill had predicted. There was going to be an accident with a man overboard.

Ronaldo was trying to push him to the rail, but Bill broke loose and used a quick kick that sent the cartel boss screaming to the deck. Chavez, physically no match for this kind of action, was backing away and found himself gripped by two of the angry gamers. A moment later he was thrown over the rail and the gamers turned their attention back to Bill.

The cartel boss now was back on his feet. One of his bodyguards had handed him a gun. Bill was again in the grip of the gamers, who were no longer sure what they were supposed to do. Ronaldo seemed ready to finish off this man who had come out of nowhere to destroy him.

He was still raising the gun when a shot rang out and a bullet passed through his neck. El Gordito was standing there with what supposedly was a useless gun. The same bodyguard who had given his weapon to Ronaldo came and gently took it from him.

Bill was standing alone. Fran had now come on the scene waving her SFPD badge and shouting that anyone still on the deck in five minutes would be under arrest. The gamers, now subdued by an actual rather than a virtual shooting, were hurrying away. Now the two Americans were alone with Paco and the three bodyguards.

Fran translated for Bill as Paco explained what had happened. He apologized that he had not done what these *agentes de policía* had told him to do. These were his friends, and he knew that they had never understood Ronaldo's goals for the cartel. Also, he knew they did not appreciate the way in which he had thrown Imelda over for the actress.

One of them was a capable gunsmith who made sure that the Browning now functioned as it should. He had also made sure there were only blanks in the gun that Ronaldo had been pointing.

It was like throwing dice, he said. Paco had not known anything more than that his gun had been fixed. Perhaps he would decide to save Bill's life by killing a man who dared do business with someone who had murdered his cousin. Perhaps he would just fire in the air as a warning and give Bill another chance to fight for his life. Perhaps he would just run from the scene.

No, Paco was not like themselves. He did not have a killer's heart. They were sure Imelda would take him back with her to Texas, and he would learn good English and maybe become a policeman. They laughed at the last part.

XXV

The sub had surfaced while they were still talking. No, there was no sign of Chavez. Some of the crew would remain on board the cruise ship while it completed its run to Ensenada. Part of the job was to convert the VR stations into more suitable family fare entertainment by replacing their taffies.

It was a chance just to be together. Bill explained that in the Air Force the post of lieutenant colonel came as officers not going any further finished their twenty years of service with duties assigned them by a colonel. He still had six months more, and he planned to be busy.

Fran accepted that while their interests had converged with neutralizing Chavez, the possibility of there being one or more individuals masterminding everything that had happened meant Bill would be working at levels definitely beyond her own skill set. As had been the case years before, they would touch each other's soul even as they touched each other's body but then put the past behind them.

Arturo could never be allowed to know the truth about his brother's death. Most likely it would be arranged that he live with his mother and his cousin as all three got past the evil that had come into their lives.

She would be home again. Already she had the premonition that murder at the O'Farrell Street playground was just an opening gambit in a game with an unseen adversary. She was the Black Queen not yet captured. She had taken out a knight if she wanted to think of Victor Chavez that way. Maybe next would be setting a bishop in motion.

Old habits die hard. At the thought Mary Francis Martinet crossed herself.

AUTHOR'S NOTE

The resemblance of my characters to individuals living or dead is purely coincidental. Since the novel is set in the future, only time will tell how much of my description of the city of San Francisco and its police department will in fact match up with reality. The same goes for the technology of VR gaming, especially in my description of taffy bars.

Writing in 2022 I have to let my imagination take over about the effects of climate change. I began my teaching career in San Francisco, described by columnist Herb Caen as Bagdad by the Bay. In five years it might be a city in the bay or possibly rebuilt over it, as is happening with Manhattan.

Obviously, I am rather negative when it comes to seeing my country move past the divisiveness resulting from the 2020 election, although I would certainly hope that my description of an annual Patriots Day dinner as well as of its guest of honor remains just a piece of satire.

There is a certain theme I am following in this book as well as its sequels. A technology that will make greed and violence obsolete does not necessarily lead to a dystopian world, but good intentions are not enough to avoid unintended consequences. Fran Martinet is very much a loose cannon. She accepts certain compromises to save the city she loves, but what she still must deal with is whether her choices will lead to its destruction.

I hope my readers are not offended by my being a white author who uses a Black woman as his principal character. In my defense I'll just say that if cultural appropriation had been a concern some years back we might never have had the pleasure of meeting James Patterson's Alex Cross.